REJECTED!

BY

OCHEI INNOCENT

MOVEMENT ONE

EXT. FRONT OF A BIG COMPOUND. -DAY

A TRADITIONAL WEDDING: ROCKINA IS PRESENTED TO THE FATHER IN-LAW. DOWRY IS PAID.

CAST:
1. CHIEF DIKE, 2. ORA THE FATHER-IN-LAW, 3. ROKINA, 4. MUSICIANS 5. CROWD.

MOVEMENT TWO

EXT. FRONT OF AN AIRPORT.

CAST;
1. CHIEF DIKE, 2. ROKINA, 3. ORA

CHIEF DIKE

My daughter, go well.

ROKINA

Amen Papa.

CHIEF DIKE

Once you settle down, remember your younger ones.

ROKINA

I will Papa.

CHIEF DIKE

I stopped your mother and siblings from being here because I do now want weeping at the airport but you have the blessings of the entire family.

ROKINA

I know Papa.

CHIEF DIKE

Then go in peace and fear nothing for America will favor you.

ROKINA

Amen.

CHIEF DIKE

My In-Law, please take care of my daughter.

ORA, [THE FATHER-IN-LAW]

It is for her protection that I am traveling with her. No shaking!

CHIEF DIKE

Thanks and journey mercies.

ORA

See you when I return.

[The two men shake hands. Chief turns and walks briskly away. Rokina hesitates for a while, picks her brief case and follows her Father-In-Law into the departure hall.]

MOVEMENT THREE

INT. A WELL POLISHED FLAT. –DAY

CAST:

1. **UNCLE, THOMAS [HUSBAND], TONY**

UNCLE

What is this I am hearing Tom?

THOMAS

What else than that my father and my new wife are arriving in three hours and I am heading to the airport with my friend Tony to receive them?

UNCLE

Is it true that you married Chief Dike's daughter?

THOMAS

Yes, the very first daughter of Chief Dike of Obuzor Village, Onicha-Olona!

UNCLE

God forbid!

THOMAS

God forbid what?

UNCLE

Not only God forbids, I forbid it!

THOMAS

Forbid what Uncle?

UNCLE

You cannot marry into such a family!

THOMAS

Why?

UNCLE

Your father just betrayed both of us and this is unforgiveable!

THOMAS

Uncle, I do not understand. Please, what is going on?

UNCLE

I will not say anything till they both arrive but just know that this so-called marriage is dead on arrival!

THOMAS

Uncle, please, kindly sit down and let me understand this.

UNCLE

I will be back in four hours to stop my brother before he brings disaster into your life.

[Storms out: Thomas collapses into a seat and holds his bowed head. Moments later Tony comes in after knocking repeatedly without answer.]

TONY

Are you so angry at my lateness as to not answer the door?

[No answer.]

Ok, I apologize.

(Takes a seat but Thomas still remains pensive. Rises after a short while.)

Ok. I get it. Your nerves are failing you! Let me get you a drink.

THOMAS

I do not need a drink Tony!

TONY

Then get hold of yourself: every man feels nervous on the first day!

THOMAS

I am not nervous Tony!

TONY

So, why are you so worried?

THOMAS

My uncle just told me that the marriage is dead on arrival.

TONY

How can he say such a thing and well after the die is cast?

THOMAS

I never dispute what my Uncle says and his counsel never fails!

TONY

But this is a different matter.

THOMAS

How is this different?

TONY

This is marriage; a lifelong project not to be taken lightly.

THOMAS

Marriage is part of destiny and my uncle has been the one leading me?

TONY

If your destiny is in the hand of your uncle, then he is your God?

THOMAS

He brought me here from a dustbin, schooled and found me a job!

TONY

Does that make him infallible?

THOMAS

He is God sent to me and a great guardian who has never been wrong.

TONY

How can he condemn a girl he has neither seen nor heard?

THOMAS

I think his grouse is with her family and not her in person.

TONY

What is with her family?

THOMAS

I have not been told: he said he will return and confront my father.

TONY

What? In the presence of the new bride?

THOMAS

I worry about two things.

TONY

What are they?

THOMAS

How the girl will feel and her reaction when I tell her no more marriage?

TONY

How can you do this, after bringing her this far? Is your mind made?

THOMAS

Yes!

TONY

Just like that?

THOMAS

I know you do not understand.

TONY

What is there to understand?

THOMAS

The words of my uncle have always been law to me.

TONY

Your decision is too hasty!

THOMAS

I know my family more than you and once my uncle has spoken even my father dare not object!

TONY

Then you have to stand up and change all that: you are not slaves!

THOMAS

You can leave Tony for I want to be alone at this moment.

TONY

Are we no more going to the airport?

THOMAS

You can go if you like: I just want to be alone.

TONY

Please, Tom, even if you are opting out of the marriage, the least we can do is to receive this girl and later sort out things.

THOMAS

My father and his brother will do the sorting.

TONY

What of your father: are you not receiving him at the airport?

THOMAS

He has been here before and he can take airport taxi.

TONY

Well, I am going to the airport: I cannot let those two be stranded.

THOMAS

I am not stopping you.

TONY

Before I go, I must urge to bear in mind that any of
your sisters can be in this ugly condition you and your
family are putting this innocent girl!

[With that he storms out. Thomas bows again with
his head in his hand.]

MOVEMENT FOUR

INT. HOTEL ROOM. –DAY

CAST:
  1. ROKINA, 2. TONY, 3. ORA

ROCKINA

Why did my husband not come to the airport?

TONY

He wants to receive you at home.

ROCKINA

And why am I being lodged in a hotel?

TONY

There is a reception in the offing to welcome you!

TOM'S FATHER

But he personally told me he would be at the airport!

TONY

There is a slight change because of the reception.

TOM'S FATHER

What concerns me with your reception?

TONY

Your elder brother will be there to plan with you.

TOM'S FATHER

So now that my daughter-in-law is settled in, can we go?

ROCKINA

And leave me alone here?

TONY

This is a reputable hotel: nothing to fear

ROKINA
What if I have a need?

TONY
Order anything: I will pick the bill and here is my number!

TOM'S FATHER

My dear daughter, I will surely see you shortly.

ROCKINA

Ok. Daddy, I will wait.

[They both leave.]

MOVEMENT FIVE

INT. TOM'S FLAT. –DAY

CAST:
1. UNCLE   2. ORA 3. TONY

UNCLE

How could you make such a mistake?

ORA [TOM'S FATHER]

Her father's lineage is not affected.

UNCLE

Says who?

TONY

What are you talking about?

UNCLE

My brother knows my second son wanted to marry into the same family.

TONY

So why did he stop?

UNCLE

If you listen to their story, you will not wish your enemy to marry into such a family!

TONY

Please tell me about it.

UNCE

It started with four brothers in the third generation of that family.

 Something happened and **the first brother** was not only paralyzed, but died prematurely, and without children.

The second brother lost two of his four sons and all males in his lineage to date are mad.

 The third brother did not have sons at all so he kept his only daughter at home to bear children in his name to stop it from closing down.

The fourth brother, who is the grandfather of this girl you have brought here, though he became the village chief, denounced idols and embraced Christianity. Yet, he lost his first son after the later had married. All his other three sons died without building a house of their own despite being senior executives. They all lost their first daughters. Two of his sons died tragically. His grand sons have been expelled from universities at one time. Randomly speaking, every two out of three girls in the family have no children and many more. Is that a family anyone would marry into with his or her eyes open? They are under a highly contagious curse.

TONY

But to every rule there is an exception!

UNCLE

Which sane person wants to take such risk when there are better options?

TONY

In this case, there is already a marriage.

UNCLE

As a lawyer, I expect you to know that every marriage contracted in error can and should be legally annulled.

TONY

I believe that since there is a chance of success, no matter how slim, we should allow them consummate this marriage.

UNCLE

I know you are not married: so if you feel so strong about this, you can go ahead and marry her. As for my Nephew, over my dead body will he go ahead! A stone seen from afar is never allowed to reach the eye, talk less of bursting it. If one finger is soiled, it reaches others sooner than later. We must protect our larger family.

ORA

I blame myself about this!

UNCLE
I wonder what came over you?

ORA

 I must have been carried away by my friendship with Chief Dike.

UNCLE

You should have known better! Put her on the next flight back to Lagos!

TONY

Why the haste Sir?

UNCLE

Tom must not set eye on her!

TONY

Excuse me sir....

UNCLE

I am done with this matter as the head of the family.

[Uncle leaves with Tony and Tom's Father still following.}

MOVEMENT SIX

INT. HOTEL ROOM. –DAY

THREE DAYS LATER.

CAST:

1. ROKINA 2. TONY

ROKINA

Look Barrister Tony, I have been in this hotel without seeing my husband!

TONY

I know but please be patient while we work out things.

ROKINA

Even my father-In-law has abandoned me.

TONY
You are not abandoned for I am here.

ROKINA
What of the man I married?

TONY
There are some developments.

ROKINA
If something is wrong, why is no one telling me what
it is?

TONY

I came today, to call a spade a spade.

ROKINA

I know already that there is a problem: just tell me
the nature of it.

TONY

Somebody came up with some shocking revelations
about your family.

ROKINA

What do you mean by that?

TONY

Some unpleasant things about your family: sort of.

ROKINA

You promised not to beat about the bush.

TONY
Yes.

ROKINA
Then hit the nail on the head please.

TONY

Stuff like premature deaths, serial barrenness and madness in the family.

ROKINA

What else is said? Please tell me!

TONY

I have a return ticket and $10,000.00 for you to go back: marriage is over.

ROKINA

The man I married did not even come to see me for a day?

TONY

He is truly devastated over the family decision.

ROKINA
He has no decision of his own?

TONY
The head of the family made him what he is today and has the say.

ROKINA

But his biological father who contracted the marriage knows my family.

TONY

His senior brother over rules and blames him for the mistake.

ROKINA

Where was this uncle when his family approached my family?

TONY

As a high profile virologist he was too busy with Covid 19 issues to even take phone calls or read letters.

ROKINA

And I am being humiliated like this by such highly educated people?

TONY

There will only be humiliation if you do not leave quietly.

ROKINA

What do I tell the villagers who danced and wished me farewell?

TONY

They will understand with time that it is no fault of yours.

ROKINA

I would rather die than go back to Nigeria with a tale like this.

TONY

Time heals all wounds please.

ROKINA

I may not weep but I have a bleeding wound in my heart.

TONY

I have to leave now.

ROKINA

Of course, if the man I married could leave me like this, what stops you?

TONY

Please, it is not like that. Tom is a good man: just family pressure.

ROKINA

Please leave before I get angry with you too! After all, you have been nice to me all this while.

TONY

I will be here in the morning to take you to the airport.

ROKINA

No problem and as you said, time heals every wound.

[Tony leaves without looking back.]

MOVEMENT SEVEN

INT. HOTEL RECEPTION. –DAY

CAST:

1. TONY 2. TWO POLICE OFFICERS 3. RECEPTIONIST

TONY

I am leaving but I would like you to keep an eye on customer in Room 21.

RECEPTIONIST

What exactly do you mean?

[She reaches her hand and presses a button.]

You are coming directly from that room, aren't you?

TONY

Yes and that is why I am giving you the information.

[Two policemen come in and stand beside Tony]

RECEPTIONIST

He tells me to keep an eye on customer in Room 21 and I do not know why!

POLICE OFFICER

Sir, did you make such request?

TONY

Yes, I did.

POLICE OFFICER

Why?

TONY

Her husband just jilted her. She came from Nigeria to see him.

POLICE OFFICER

Do you have any form of identification?

TONY

Yes please. Here are my papers.

[Hands the officer his documents.]

POLICE OFFICER

You are an attorney?

TONY

And the one who checked her in here.

POLICE OFFICER

Sorry but you have to wait while we confirm her wellbeing before your leave.

TONY

No problem.

[The officer goes away and returns in few minutes.]

POLICE OFFICER

Ok, you can go Sir while we keep an eye on her.

TONY

Thanks and I will be here in the morning to take her to the airport.

RECEPTIONIST

You are welcome.

[Tony leaves.]

MOVEMENT EIGHT

INT. HOTEL RECEPTION. –DAY

CAST:

1. TONY 2. RECEPTIONIST

RECEPTION

Sorry, Attorney your friend left two hours ago.

TONY

What?

RECEPTIONIST

She left.

TONY

To the airport?

RECEPTIONIST

She did not say but left this note for you.

[Hands him a sealed envelope. He opens and reads aloud.]

TONY

"Thanks Barrister Tony. My heart is heavy but not so much as not to appreciate your kindness to me. Since I cannot bear the shame of returning to Nigeria immediately, I have decided to keep moving as God leads, hoping that I will soon go far enough as not to remember what just happened.

May our paths never meet again because that will reopen my wounds.

Please, find enclosed: the $10,000.00 and return ticket. I may not have money, but I have self respect. I cannot take money from such filthy people.

Do whatever you like with the money because your kindness to me merits it.

Bye.

Rokina Dike."

RECEPTIONIST

She wept as she left.

TONY

Which way did she go?

RECEPTIONIST

The taxi was waiting as she came down so I did not hear her destination.

TONY

Do you have the number of the taxi?

RECEPTIONIST

Yes, our CCTV must have captured it.

TONY

Please get it for me: I must track and help her.

RECEPTIONIST

Ok. Give me two minutes.

[Receptionist leaves and returns with a piece of paper. Tony thanks her and leaves.]

MOVEMENT NINE

INT. CHURCH OFFICE. –DAY

SIX MONTHS LATER.

CAST:

1. PASTOR 2. TONY

PASTOR

Your look Tony, tells me you have not found her.

TONY

That is the painful truth.

PASTOR

You have to face other things now.

TONY

How can I?

PASTOR

Why not?

TONY

Her visa expires this week: now she will be running from the law!

PASTOR

That is if she is not yet in custody.

TONY

The detective I hired searched all the hospitals, prisons and homes.

PASTOR

She might have left the country.

TONY

To where? She did not have enough money.

PASTOR

Well, you have no guilt since you are not the one who brought her here!

TONY

I have made a decision to go to Nigeria.

PASTOR

What for?

TONY

Her memory haunts me and her money is still in my account!

PASTOR

But her letter clearly willed the money to you.

TONY

I have enough of my own.

PASTOR

I can see that you are determined.

TONY

The least I can do is trace her family in Nigeria.

PASTOR

You were born in America: have you been to Nigeria before?

TONY

Once: with my parents.

PASTOR

It is a risky thing to do at a time like this.

TONY

You taught us to be of help to people.

PASTOR

I can see your mind is really made.

TONY

I have purchased my ticket.

PASTOR

You know how to trace the family?

TONY

I have done some digging: Thomas also told me a lot about his village.

PASTOR

Thank God that being of African origin, you can mingle easily.

TONY

Yes and I plan to dress like other Africans.

PASTOR

 So when are you leaving?

TONY

Two days time!

PASTOR

Then kneel let us pray.

[And they began to pray. Suddenly, pastor stops and begins to speak in tongues.]

PASTOR

The Lord says I should go with you and that he will do a new thing in Africa through this trip.

TONY

Are you sure Pastor?

PASTOR

Once the Lord spoke but twice did I hear.

TONY

Are you really coming with me?

PASTOR

When the Lord says a thing, who am I to argue?

[Tony jumps with joy and embraces the pastor.]

TONY

I better run along and buy the extra ticket before it is too late.

PASTOR

I will use this period to set up a team to pray from now till we return.

TONY

Wow! God I thank you for this! And thank God you are also African.

PASTOR

Yes. That makes mingling relatively easier.

TONY

Wow! I can't believe this!

PASTOR

Please run along, I have some administrative duties to delegate!

TONY

I am off!

[Tony runs out, still shouting for joy.]

MOVEMENT TEN

EXT. AIRPORT. –DAY

TONY AND PASTOR ARE SEEN ENTERING THE AIRPORT DEPARTURE HALL. AIRCRAFT IS SEEN TAKING OFF.

CAST:

1. PASTOR   2.TONY

MOVEMENT ELEVEN

INT. CHIEF DIKE'S HOME. –DAY

CAST:

1. CHIEF DIKE 2. TONY 3. PASTOR. 4. TWO POLICE OFFICERS.

CHIEF DIKE

If I heard you right, you brought $10,000.00 belonging to my daughter and to tell me that the man who took my daughter to her son after marrying her according to our native law and custom threw her into the streets and for the past six months, nobody knows the where about of my daughter?

TONY

Unfortunately, that is so Sir.

CHIEF DIKE

I want you to know that since they left with my daughter, neither the man who took her nor my daughter has called me and that is more than six months now.

TONY

That is not fair at all. We hoped she might have contacted you somehow.

CHIEF DIKE

Nothing like that! Please give me a moment: I have something to do inside.

TONY

Ok Sir.

[Chief leaves.]

PASTOR

I sense danger Tony but the Lord is in control.

TONY

Danger?

PASTOR

Danger but the Lord says remain calm.

[At that moment, chief returns.]

CHIEF DIKE

I do not want to take laws into my hand but I am afraid I have to hand both of you over to the police.

TONY

Police?

CHIEF DIKE

You are the only contact I have to those who sold my daughter.

TONY

Sold? I never said she was sold.

CHIEF DIKE

Then what is the money for?

[Two armed policemen enter.]

CHIEF DIKE

These are the two men who sold my daughter.

POLICE OFFICER

Please, follow us to the station. You have a right to remain silent because whatever you say henceforth shall be used against you in court.

PASTOR

We are willing to follow you.

POLICE OFFICER

Then, let's go.

[They all leave.]

MOVEMENT TWELVE

EXT. ROKINA'S FATHER-IN-LAW'S COMPOUND. - DAY

Youths are seen vandalizing the compound till police comes to disperse them.

CAST:

1. **YOUTHS**   3. **POLICE OFFICERS**

MOVEMENT THIRTEEN

INT. POLICE STATION. –DAY

CAST:

1. **INSPECTOR** 2. **DPO** 3. **SECRETARY** 4. **PASTOR** 5. **TONY**

INSPECTOR

Sir, since those two men got here, the cells have been on fire.

DIVISIONAL POLICE OFFICER [DPO]

Even the entire city is on fire.

INSPECTOR

Needless to say that our men are over stretched containing the rampaging youths of Chief Dike's village and that of his in-law.

DPO

Do you have more details on the feud?

INSPECTOR

Chief Dike's youths allege that Dike's In-law took his daughter and sold her and that the two men in our cell brought the price money to him.

DPO

And what do the men say for themselves?

INSPECTOR

They are asking for legal representation and getting their phones back to enable them call the American Embassy.

DPO

Why did you not tell me they are American citizens?

INSPECTOR

I just found out.

DPO

Bring them to my office immediately.

INSPECTOR

Yes Sir!

DPO

First, send my secretary in!

INSPECTOR

Yes Sir!

[Inspector goes out and Secretary comes in immediately.]

SECRETARY

Morning Sir!

DPO

Easy! I want my next session recorded. I did not need to tell you that but I am just taking the precaution of asking you to make sure nothing goes wrong.

SECRETARY

Yes Sir!

DPO

You may go.

[Secretary salutes and exits as Inspector returns with Tony and Pastor.]

INSPECTOR

The two suspects are here Sir!

DPO

Gentlemen, please be seated.

[They do.]

Please tell me your own side of the story. I must warn that you are being recorded and you have a right to remain silent.

PASTOR

I am Pastor Andy Barnabas of New Pentecost Church, Houston, Florida and we are here under the leading of God to help Chief' Dike's family. My colleague is

Barrister Tony with a going practice in the same city and a staunch member of our ministry.

DPO

We have $10.000.00 kept with us by Chief Dike as evidence that his daughter was sold to you.

TONY

That is far from the truth.

DPO

Please tell me all you know about this issue that has led to a communal clash.

TONY

When I saw the way things were going, I thought it wise to record as much of my discussions with everyone in US both to protect myself and preserve the truth. As a lawyer, I knew this might be needed one day.

DPO

You have a tape recording of everything?

TONY

Even our ongoing discussion is being recorded.

DPO

Ok. We know technology has gone far: can I have a copy of the tape?

TONY

In two minutes Sir.

[Tony rubs his stomach.]

Done Sir! It is in your android phone as well as the official records of this office.

DPO

Thanks. Inspector, take them back to the cell. I will send for them after I have listened to the tape.

PASTOR

We want to talk with the American Embassy.

DPO

Why did you not use the same method you used to transfer info to me?

TONY

The embassy number is on my phone but the recorded information is on cloud and I can get it out anywhere with the remote I have in my button.

DPO

I see. Let them have their phones and keep them in your office instead.

INSPECTOR

Yes Sir.

[Inspector exits with both men.]

MOVEMENT FOURTEEN

INT. DPO'S OFFICE. –DAY

CAST:

1. DPO 2. CHIEF DIKE 3. CHIEF OZAH 4. ELDERS

DPO
My fathers, I have brought you together because we have a delicate situation on hand.

CHIEF DIKE
Living itself is delicate.

CHIEF OZAH
My worry is why Chief Dike who admitted sending boys to vandalize houses in my village is still here a free man while innocent boys are languishing in your cell for protecting their properties.

CHIEF DIKE
I sent no one to vandalize. I only told my youths what happened to their sister. Can you ride the back of a tiger and expect to remain alive?

CHIEF OZAH
You have put your hand in the mouth of a viper.

DPO
I have called you here to listen to a tape recording of
what happened in America from the day Chief Dike's
daughter reached America.

[The elders react variously while the DPO turns on
the tape. Everyone listens with rapt attention.]

MOVEMENT FIFTEEN

INT. INSPECTOR'S OFFICE –DAY

CAST:

1. INSPECTOR 2. TONY 3. PASTOR 3. SECRETARY 4. EMBASSY ATTACHE

INSPECTOR

We got signal from the State Police HQ that a representative of your Ambassador will be with us in a matter of minutes. Please read and sign these papers so that when he comes you can go with him back to Lagos.

PASTOR

That is not what we requested for!

INSPECTOR

What did you request for?

PASTOR

How can we leave when we have not started our mission?

INSPECTOR

Do you know that this station might come under attack any time?

PASTOR

We did not travel all the way here just to chicken out at the least threat!

INSPECTOR

These are no empty threats Pastor.

PASTOR

All the same, we intend to stay: our God is well able to protect.

TONY

We only asked for the recommendation of a worthy legal representative

[At that moment, there is siren]

INSPECTOR

I think that should be your man: the siren is certainly not ours.

TONY

Please, we do not intend to leave yet.

PASTOR

We have a mission to accomplish!

[Presently, Secretary comes in with the Embassy Attaché. They all rise to exchange pleasantries.]

ATTACHE
Gentle men, we are going home.

PASTOR
Your Excellency, we are not able to go with you.

ATTACHE
What are you talking about? I am here to post the bail
bond.

[DPO comes in. Inspector chests out.]

INSPECTOR
This is my boss.

[DPO and Attaché exchange greetings.]

ATTACHE
I have come to take these men.

DPO
That would not be necessary.

ATTACHE
Why?

DPO
I have restored peace with the warring chiefs. Please
follow me to meet them.

[They follow him out.]

MOVEMENT SIXTEEN

INT. POLICE STATION CONFERENCE ROOM. – DAY

CAST:

1. DPO 2. METU 3. CHIEF DIKE 4. CHIEF OZAH 5. ATTACHE 6. PASTOR 7. TONY

DPO
I greet you high chiefs.

CHIEFS
We greet you too.

DPO
I went out to get the two visitors to this land and met the representative of the US Embassy in Nigeria in the Inspector's office. He was posting bail for them but I told him that would not be necessary since we have already resolved the issue. Have we not?

CHIEFS
We have.

DPO
Barrister Tony thoughtfully made a video tape of all
the transactions in America and merely watching the
video was enough to convince both parties that the
fight was uncalled for.

CHIEF OZAH
I still say what my brother did to Dike's daughter is
not in our character and I would have reacted worse
than Dike did. All our youths will be angry with him.

CHIEF DIKE
They should leave him to me.

DPO
Thank God for helping us nib the crisis in the bud.

ATTACHE

So why were my men arrested in the first place?

DPO
They were accused of slavery and human trafficking.
Thank God we took them in because we do not know
what would have happened if the youths had met
them on the street in their moments of anger.

PASTOR
Praise God for His intervention.

ATTACHE
Can I go with them now?

DPO
That is theirs to decide. They are very welcome here
now that this matter is solved.

PASTOR
We shall stay: we want to minister to the family of
Chief Dike.

TONY
We heard stories of long histories of madness,
barrenness, etc and when I could not find Rokina, I
said the least I could do is bring the money to her
family and seek out pastors that can pray out the
family!

OZAH

**Chief Dike's ancestry is a lineage of warriors
and there is no great warrior that does not
come under a curse or two at one time or the
other.**
DPO
At first, I did not believe the tape and the things I
heard. So I went to the oldest man in the village to
ask him if the Dike Family is under curse and how it
happened.

PASTOR
What did the old man say?

DPO
I did not get the details but I was satisfied with his
confirmation.

TONY
Can you take us to him? We need to hear the story to
know how to go about it all.

DPO
I brought this old man here to help me stop these two
chiefs from fighting.

PASTOR
 The same man that confirmed the history we are
after?

METU

I witnessed it all and I remember how it all started. I
see it as clearly as yesterday.

[Flashback.]

MOVEMENT SEVENTEEN

INT. FLASH BACK TO THE KING'S PALACE HUNDRED YEARS AGO. –DAY

CAST:

1. AGU 2. KING 3. IKE 4.ISAMA 5. PASSIVE ELDERS

AGU

I remind you again that the white man is preparing another war against us.

KING

And I know that you too are preparing: not so?

AGU

We resisted him for thirty-one years because we prepared well.

KING

Is anything hampering your preparation?

AGU

We have always fought from two fronts: I on one side and the War Leader on the other side.

KING

Obuzor Village has yet to present a War Leader.

AGU

I need your permission to step up and become the War Leader.

IKE

What nonsense are you talking about Agu?

AGU

If not that we are before the king, I would have beheaded you for talking while I am talking.

IKE

I may be old but do not forget that a man cannot be too old for a dance he knows too well. Before an idiot like you can lift his hand, you will be dead.

KING

Stop that two of you. Do you know where you are?

IKE

Sorry, Your Highness: Imagine this power drunk rat poking his hands into my eyes! Is it because I am old?

KING

If I hear either of you again, I will have you executed.

ISAMA

But the matter is really serious. This clan cannot continue without a War Leader.

IKE

Has my clan ever failed to present a War Leader?

ISAMA

But this is our seventh year of waiting. The *Ekwumekwu* war may be over but what if there is a second wave especially now that our troops are greatly reduced?

KING

Actually, we need a War Leader. Chief Ike, what is the problem? Is there a shortage of capable men in your family?

IKE

No matter how many elephants drink from it, the sea can never dry up.

KING

We have been through all this before and I understand how Agu feels.

AGU

I speak for other generals and warriors as well.

KING

I hereby decree that Obuzor village is given seven days to present a War Leader or forfeit the position to the next in command. Our army cannot continue without a head.

IKE

You have spoken well oh King and I assure you that we shall present a war leader within the set period.

KING

In that case, I shall rise to meet with my Queen.

[They all rise while the king goes into the inner recess.]

MOVEMENT EIGHTEEN

FLASH BACK. EXT. FRONT OF IKE'S HOUSE. – DAY

CAST:

1. **IKE 2. UBA 3. NTU 4. NDU. 5. PASSIVE ELDERS**

IKE
Great people of Obuzor village, I greet you all.

ALL
Yaaah!

IKE
Some of you might have heard that the king made a decree today.

NTU
Something like that entered my ear this morning.

IKE
For those of us who like pretending that walls do not have ears, I announce officially that the King has given us only seven days to present a War Leader.

UBA

But we have already chosen a War Leader.

NTU

The only thing holding us is that we do not have a lion's skin and lion's blood for the rituals.

NDU

Our hunters have combed the forests from here to Asaba but no lion in sight.

IKE

Our enemies know that and they are beginning to mock us with it.

UBA

There must be a way out.

IKE

You may have heard too that I promised the king that we will present the War Leader in seven days!

NTU

How can you make such a promise when we have been searching for lions all this while?

IKE

Our people say, when you do not know what to do, you do what you know.

UBA

Is there anything we know in this case?

IKE

We shall use our magic rope.

ALL
Ah!

NTU
But that is used only in situations of war.

UBA
And it is always used against invaders only.

IKE
Are we not at war? Did you see how Agu attacked me?

NTU
We were waiting let him behead you let us see what will happen to his family.

UBA
I said nothing but my cutlass was within reach.

IKE
Yet, did I not hear someone hear say that we have no enemy?

NTU
Agu is an enemy within.

IKE
Who will go and drop it in on their road to the farm?

UBA
I will.

IKE
Then, as the oldest man, I shall bring out the magic rope tonight.

UBA

The first male to walk over it becomes a lion.

NTU

Why did we not do this since?

IKE

There was no ultimatum then and we hoped to naturally find a lion in the bush.

NTU

Can I go with him to shoot the lion?

IKE

You cannot shoot in Agu's village without attracting avoidable trouble.

NTU

Just tell me where to find the lion.

IKE

All should be done at six o'clock in the morning. The first brave man to visit the farm will walk over it and appear where we want him to appear.

NTU

You have not told me where to ambush the lion: is it on their farm road?

IKE

Wait under the first mango tree on our own farm road. It shall appear there by invocation. Take a strong warrior with you: lions can take more than a blow.

NTU
My father killed a lion with bare hands have you
forgotten?

IKE
Take another person with you just in case. Good
night all.

[They all leave.]

MOVEMENT NINETEEN

FLASHBACK.   EXT. FARM ROAD. –NIGHT

Uba is seen dodging a sentry before placing a rope on the road. He melts into the night.

CAST:

1.   **UBA 2. SENTRY.**

MOVEMENT TWENTY

FLASH BACK. EXT. FARM ROAD. –DAY.

Ntu is seen with Aka as they position themselves under a mango tree.

CAST:

  1. NTU 2. AKA

NTU
I shall aim for its head: I want to shoot only once.

AKA

If for any reason, you miss, I shall aim for its left hand for that is what most cats attack with.
NTU
I cannot miss and from what Pa Ike said, the lion should not take long in appearing here.

[At that moment, a lion appears.]

NTU
The devil is here and starring at me!

[He releases a shot. The lion falls and so too does Ntu. Aka is confused for a moment but he gathers himself and beheads the lion with a blow of his machete. Next, he cuts off the tail and collects the blood in a gourd.]

AKA

Elder brother! Rise for the deed is done!

[No response.]

Rise for we have not only lion blood but its skin.

[No response. Aka takes a close look at Ntu.]

AKA

No! You cannot be paralyzed! It is not possible.

[He hits him with a charm Ntu opens his eyes but is not able to talk.]

I shall have to carry you and run for time is of essence. He picks up Ntu and runs home!]

MOVEMENT TWENTY-ONE

FLASHBACK. FRONT OF AGU'S HOUSE. -DAY

CAST:

1. AGU   2. UDE   3. THREE ELDERS 4. PASSIVE ADULTS

AGU

I called you here because a witch cried yesterday and today the baby died.

UDE

Ike's people could not get a lion's skin for years only for them to produce one overnight. Something is not normal.

AGU

On top of that one of our strongest warriors went out early yesterday and up to now, he is still missing.

UDE
If you are thinking what I am thinking, then we have to take action.

AGU
Ike can do anything just to spite me; yet we have to be sure first.

UDE
There can be no other explanation and for that I say to arms!

AGU
We must consult the oracles first and be sure or fight a war of blame.

UDE
We are warriors and warriors shoot first and ask questions later.

AGU
I sent three elders yesterday night to the great oracle of Obamkpa.

UDE
And what did the oracle say?

AGU
I called this meeting in anticipation of their return.

UDE
For too long, our village has played second fiddle to Obuzor. This is our chance to change everything.

AGU

If it turns out to be what I think, then blood shall
flow.

[Three elders walk in.]

1ST ELDER

The people with whom we eat in the same plate have
stabbed us in the back.

AGU

Call a spade a spade: this is not a time for parables.

2ND ELDER

Before we could even speak, the oracle told us how it
all happened.

AGU

Tell us how it happened so that we know how to
respond.

1ST ELDER

They used their notorious magic rope, which they
placed on our farm road and our brother walked over
it and turned to a lion which they killed and skinned
for their rituals.

[All began to talk at once. Some drew their machetes
and sprang to their feet]

AGU

Silence!

3RD ELDER
Vexed as we are, we must all consider what the oracle said further.

AGU
Sit down everybody so we can hear and decide how to dance.

3RD ELDER
The oracle counseled that since the lion that ate our goat is readily waiting for the owner to react, we should change our tactics.

[Another uproar.]

AGU
Quiet! We sent them so we must hear them out.

UDE
What else can they say than that we should not fight?

AGU
Let them have their say and we will decide for ourselves how to chew the bone.

3RD ELDER
The oracle said we should deal with them with a weapon similar to theirs!

UDE
What is that and how painful is it?

3RD ELDER
The oracle gave us this powder.

[She unties her wrapper and all crane their necks to see it.]

UDE
What for? Are we to beautify our enemies?

3RD ELDER
Trust me: they told us what to do in secret.

UDE
Secret?

3RD ELDER
Yes, in secret: only the three of us and two warriors will witness it dead in the night.

AGU
To what effect is my question?

3RD ELDER
The moment we do what has to be done, the person Obuzor is presenting will run mad for all eyes to see. Secondly, there will be no more war leaders from that village because a mad man cannot be allowed to lead our clan to war.

[Uproar.]

AGU
How will that be?

3RD ELDER
How will they be able to present a war leader when all their first sons are mad?

[Uproar.]

UDE
Can't their second sons take over?

3RD ELDER
All other sons will become aimless loafers and wanderers. Can any person who has not built a house be War Leader in this clan?

ALL
No!

3RD ELDER
To prevent their sisters from helping them, the oracle says all their sisters shall not only bury their first children but shall thereafter be barren. Above all, no matter how good their behavior, attitude or labor, they shall be sent back to their fathers!

AGU
So we shall henceforth be the War Leaders?

1ST ELDER
The answer is a big "Yes".

AGU
Then, what are we waiting for? Go and do what needs to be done.

UDE
Yes. Their folly has served us well.

[And they all leave.]

MOVEMENT TWENTY-TWO

INT. DPO'S OFFICE. –DAY

CAST:

1. DPO 2. METU 3. PASTOR 4. TONY
5.CHIEF OZAH 6. CHIEF DIKE 7.
EMBASSY ATTACHE

METU

My mother was among the three that went on that errand for Chief Agu and according to her, that is how the curse was laid upon Obuzor Village.

DPO

I have been serving in this town for over three years now. Obuzor Village is quite large. Why Dike family alone?

METU

Hundred years ago, there were only four brothers and their extended families. Some strangers relocated to

Obuzor Village because they felt that living with the war leader gives them more security. Most of the residents of Obuzor today are descendants of strangers and settlers.

PASTOR
Can you give us some more information on the four brothers and their descendants?

METU
Ntu who shot the lion became not only paralyzed on the spot but got his lineage shut down because no male child has been born thereafter. Aka who bled the lion lost all his sons before he died. Uba, who dropped the rope gave birth to only a girl. Only the descendants of Ike, who is the grandfather of Chief Dike here survived because Ike was a great medicine man.

CHIEF DIKE
Yet, my immediate father had five sons but only I survived and none could build a house before dying. I inherited my father's house. Apart from one or two random exceptions, the curse has been very effective. The few males who survived, after being born mainly via concubines, are mad.

CHIEF OZAH
I repeat that it was not enough for Dike's daughter to be treated the way she was by my family abroad. What if her case is one of the rare exceptions?

PASTOR
Thank God that both families now have responsible
and informed leaders.

DPO
I thank God too because now, we can all hold hands
and find a solution to the lingering issue.

TONY
I appeal to two of you to please, for the sake of the
girl, come together and let's find a solution.

PASTOR
We are not searching for a solution: the Bible has
already made clear what we shall do in such a
circumstance.

CHIEF OZAH
I believe it is not by accident that you and my brother
became close friends despite the age long coldness
between our two villages.

CHIEF DIKE
I did not even remember such because all my years as
you can recall, I was in the army and was busy
travelling with the army to different war theatres. I
only returned when my father died.

CHIEF OZAH
The fact that you survived all the wars you were in
must have made many assume that you and your
nuclear family are exceptions to the curse.

PASTOR
Two of you should gather representatives of all families involved on both sides for a reconciliation starting from tomorrow and it shall last for three days, during which no one should eat or drink.

CHIEF OZAH
Though I am not a Christian, I shall cooperate in full because I want this issue to end.

DPO
I shall not only participate, but provide all needed security.

CHIEF DIKE
I pledge my commitment to whatever you want to do but I still ask for my daughter.

ATTACHE
I am so happy to be a witness to this and I assure you chief that as I return to the embassy, we shall send relevant signals home and your daughter will be found. I also believe in prayers: meaning that God will help find her.

PASTOR
Amen. He will.

TONY
Thanks so much for being here Sir.

ATTACHE
Uncle Sam will do that for you any day and anywhere. I beg to leave and just call if and when you need me.

[They all rise and go out with him.]

MOVEMENT TWENTY-THREE

EXT. FRONT OF THE POLICE STATION. –DAY

They watch the Attaché's Orderly opens door, Attaché enters and Driver zooms off.

CAST:
  1. DPO 2. PASTOR 3. TONY 4. ATTACHE 5. DRIVER 6. ORDERLY

DPO
He should be able to catch the last flight from Asaba to Lagos.

PASTOR
I pray he does.

DPO
I guess you are checking back into the hotel? I will give you two guards though you are not in any danger.

PASTOR
We prefer to remain in the police cell.

DPO
What?

PASTOR
We made some in-mates our prayer partners: we
need them now.

DPO
Let me tell you what I will do: I will find out those
whose offences are bail able and ask them to post
bail. That way, they can follow you to the hotel or a
local church for your fasting and prayer.

TONY
We equally can do with collaboration with local
churches.

DPO
I know the local chairman of the National Christians
Association. I will talk with him and probably ask him
to see you in the hotel.

PASTOR
Thanks so much: we need as many more as can, not
only join us in fasting and prayer but are well able to
do house to house evangelism during these three
days.

DPO
I have no doubt that the local churches will be
delighted to help.

TONY
Thanks for your help so far.

[They shake hands and the two depart.]

MOVEMENT TWENTY-FOUR

EXT. VILLAGE SQUARE. –DAY

THREE DAYS LATER: A LARGE CROWD IS GATHERED. POLICEMEN ARE SEEN AT STRATEGIC POINTS.

CAST:

1. PASTOR 2. TONY 3. POLICE OFFICERS 4. CHIEF DIKE 5. CHIEF OZAH 6. CROWD. 7. ROKINA 8. ROSE 9. CROWD. 10. KING.

PASTOR

Our Lord our God and Father, your Word says is 2 chronicles 7:14 that:
"if my people, who are called by my name, will humble themselves and pray and seek my face and turn from their wicked ways, then I will hear from heaven, and I will forgive their sin and will heal their land."

We seek your face this day as a people. Hear Oh God and heal our land!

ALL
Amen!

PASTOR
Can Chief Dike please come forward to apologize and ask for forgiveness in behalf of your ancestors for the Word of God says in the Bible book of James 5:16: ***"Therefore confess your sins to each other and pray for each other so that you may be healed. The prayer of a righteous person is powerful and effective."?***

CHIEF DIKE
I Chief Dike, being the most senior surviving member of the Obuzor Village, hereby renounce the sins of my ancestors in generally and particularly over the person turned into a lion to enable my family present a War Leader to the King about a hundred years ago. I apologize and ask for the forgiveness from the indigenes of Umuagu Village.

PASTOR
Can Chief Ozah please come forward and renounce the sins of his own people.

CHIEF OZAH
I renounce the sins of our ancestors as a people from Umuagu Village, for paying evil for evil and causing hardship for innocent and unborn children and other sins too numerous to mention. I also apologize to the

people of Obuzor Village and all other people that our actions must have offended.

PASTOR
Please, let everyone here repeat this prayer after me: We as a people, hereby renounce all gods of vengeance and bloodshed that have kept us captive over these years.

[All repeat.]

PASTOR
From this day forward we accept Jesus Christ, the Prince of Peach as our personal Lord and Savior even as we pledge to henceforth live in peace with one another.

[They all repeat.}

PASTOR
I beg the two chiefs to please embrace one another.

[They obey.]

PASTOR
I now call on His Royal Highness the King to please say a word of prayer.

KING
Jehovah God of all creations, please accept the confessions and prayers of our people today. As king over this land, I decree that all curses are broken and at end from today henceforth. Anyone who attempts to renew them, let the curse follow him or her alone.

ALL
Amen!

PASTOR
In closing this Solemn Assembly Lord, we thank you for being here for your Word says where two or three are gathered in your name, you are always there. Thank you for helping us this far! Lord, we pray also that Chief's daughter be found so that our joy be full: thank you for healing this land and we know by faith that peace will reign henceforth in this land. May...

ROSE
Chief! Chief! Chief!!

[There is commotion as people turn to stare at the direction of the calls. Soon Rose comes into view pushed and edged forward by the crowd.]

PASTOR
Who is she?

ROSE
Chief Dike, Rokina is here!

CHIEF DIKE
What?

OZAH
Who is Rokina?

[A huge cry rents the air and some youths come forward, carrying Rokina high above all heads. They stand her in front of Chief Dike who collapses. Police cordon the altar and whisk away all on it. Some of

those left behind are rejoicing while others are asking
questions.]

MOVEMENT TWENTY-FIVE

INT. HOTEL ROOM. –DAY

THREE DAYS LATER

CAST:

1. ROKINA 2. TONY 3. PASTOR.

ROKINA
Believe it: It took my father a full day to accept that I am the one.

TONY
He really thought you were dead and I really thank God for our first chance to talk one on one. Were you avoiding me?

ROKINA
Why? I was so busy helping my father recover and what with so many visitors. I was really overwhelmed. The churches kept up with more prayers for my family and my father in particular.

TONY

So how did you hear of our Solemn Assembly?

ROKINA

My only school mate and friend in this town Rose called me and told me the whole town had gone into a three day fasting for me.

TONY

When did you return and how did Rose get to know of your arrival in the country since you kept everyone in the dark?

ROKINA

I was too ashamed and never wanted anyone to know I had been deported in addition to being jilted by the person who married me but my heart was so heavy that I decided to call Rose who had been a close childhood friend and confidant.

TONY

Thank God for that: otherwise no one would have known you were in Nigeria.

ROKINA

I felt a leading by God to call her despite my resolve not to call or contact anyone. My suffering and experience, pushed me closer to God in the US. I spent most of the time in a church with old people's home where I cleaned the floor till one day somebody asked for my papers.

Staying in church gave me time to pray and know God. On returning to Nigeria, I diligently searched for a church where they had activities regularly and slept there with others I guess had housing problems too.

TONY
Your matter drove me closer to God too and I began to visit Pastor more. And later, I decided to come and hand the $10,000.00 to your parents. I also hoped to pray with them and ask whether they had any information on you.

ROKINA

You took a big risk.

TONY
Just as you took a big risk marrying a man you had never met before.

ROKINA
When are you going back to the US?

TONY
Can I offer you a job in my office?

ROKINA
What?

TONY
I need a PA in my office in Houston.

ROKINA
Are you trying to reconcile me and your friend?

TONY
No.

ROKINA

You do not need to pity me: I thank God for it all because if not for the experience, I would not have met Christ.

TONY

And if not for that, I would not have met you.

[They sit silent for a while.]

ROKINA

The first thing my father did this morning was to return the dowry he received to Tom's family.

TONY

I also know that Tom's uncle filed for divorce on his behalf and got an accelerated annulment within a month of your disappearance.

[They sit still for some moment. Tony goes to his knees.]

TONY

Rokina, will you marry me?

ROKINA

[Goes into his arm sniffing.]

Back then when I was in that hotel, you were so kind that I could not help falling in love with you. Moreover, when you came to the airport, my spirit leapt when I saw you for I felt you were my husband only to be told you were not.

TONY
Can we have a quiet wedding in Nigeria before returning to the US?

PASTOR
[Walks in.]

Sorry. I was by the window. Why not in this small town with the DPO and all the chiefs as witnesses?

TONY
With Rose as bride's maid and the Embassy Attaché as Special Guest of honor?

PASTOR
My sister, can I tell you a secret?

ROKINA
Please tell me Pastor.

PASTOR
From the day Brother Tony began to talk of you in my office, I noticed an abnormal sparkle in his eyes and I realized that he would never be ok unless we find you.

[And they all laughed long.]

MOVEMENT TWENTY-SIX

INT. CHIEF DIKE'S HOUSE. –DAY.

TEN YEARS LATER!

CAST:

   1. TONY 2. ROKINA 3. CHIEF DIKE 4. JUNIOR 5. THREE OTHER KIDS.

TONY
Daddy, it is good to see you after such a long time.

CHIEF DIKE
But I was in US just last year.

TONY
Your grandchildren were crying for you so I brought all four of them to see you. To us it is like ten years ago that you visited.

ROKINA
That is not the only reason we came.

CHIEF DIKE
What is the other reason?

ROKINA
Our tenth wedding anniversary comes up in three days time and we decided to celebrate it here in a grand style!

CHIEF DIKE
Ten years you say?

TONY
Yes Daddy. Ten years!

CHIEF DIKE
How time flies and the king will be happy to see you because he told me he would like to confer a chieftaincy title on you for your donations and scholarships to youths of the town.

TONY
Me a chief? Wow! Junior did you hear that?

JUNIOR
An African chief? I am sure you will look ugly with white chalk on your face!

[All but Junior laugh long.]

THE END.

OTHER NOVELS AND SCREENPLAYS BY THE SAME AUTHOR

1. THE BANISHED PASTOR
2. LIKE FATHER LIKE SON
3. STUPID GIRLS
4. HUNTED ON ALL SIDES
5. THE POMPOUS CHIEF
6. THE RISE OF DIGIDOM
7. THE SAD STORY OF MRS HEN. COCK

ABOUT THE AUTHOR

OCHEI INNOCENT, A JOURNALIST AND CLERGYMAN LOVES TELLING STORIES MORE THAN FOOD.

HIS BOOKS DELIBERATELY AIMS TO SOLVE ONE PROBLEM IN THE LIFE OF THE READER IN ANDDITION TO ENTERTAINING.

ABOUT THE BOOK

ROKINA IS SENT TO USA AFTER BEING MARRIED BY PROXY IN AN AFRICAN COUNTRY. THE HUSBAND COMES NEITHER TO THE AIRPORT ON HER ARRIVAL, WHICH HE ARRANGED NOR IS THERE A PHONE CALL. ROKINA CANNOT BE TRACED FOR SIX MONTHS. A MISSION GOES OUT IN SEARCH OF HER. IT CREATES A CITY-WIDE RIOT IN HER HOME TOWN AND BOTH GOVERNMENTS GET INVOLVED.